For Carl ~ C.F.

For Sarah, Chris and Hannah ~ S.M.

This edition published by Scholastic Inc., 557 Broadway; New York, NY 10012,
by arrangement with Little Tiger Press.
SCHOLASTIC and associated logos are trademarks and/or registered trademarks of Scholastic Inc.
Scholastic Canada Ltd.; Markham, Ontario

First published in the United States by Good Books, Intercourse, PA 17534, 2007

Library of Congress Cataloging-in-Publication Data is available for this title.

Original edition published in English by Little Tiger Press,
an imprint of Magi Publications, London, England, 2007.

Text copyright © Claire Freedman 2007
Illustrations copyright © Simon Mendez 2007

All rights reserved. No part of this book may be reproduced in any manner,
except for brief quotations in critical articles or reviews, without permission.

ISBN 13: 978-1-84506-604-8
ISBN 10: 1-84506-604-9

Printed in China

2 4 6 8 10 9 7 5 3 1

I Love You, Sleepyhead

Claire Freedman   Simon Mendez

Look, little child,
as the night is unfurled,
The animals are going to bed
all around the world.

Close to her mother
and safe by her side,
Sweet little fawn
is so sleepy-eyed.

Nestled in grass,
as the soft breezes blow,
Bathed by the warmth
of the sun's evening glow.

Lion cubs romp as the sun slips away.
In the soft golden light, there's still time to play.

Soon they'll be yawning, three tired sleepyheads,
Watched by their mother all night in their beds.

Waddling to mommy,
the tired ducklings quack,
Sleepy from swimming,
they're glad to be back.

Safely they're tucked
in their nest for the night,
Feathery bundles,
huddled up tight.

Daylight is fading fast, softly dusk falls.
"Bedtime, my little ones," mother fox calls.

"Mom, we're not sleepy!" the small foxes cry,
As low in the sky, the sun says goodbye.

Wrapped up in love,
little bear feels so snug,
Cuddled goodnight
in a big mommy-hug.

Drifting to sleep
he sinks into her fur,
Warm in the soft snow,
snuggled with her.

High up, the trees catch the last rays of sun,
As three tired monkeys climb up to their mom.

The sounds of the jungle, the rustling of leaves,
Lull them to sleep in the cool evening breeze.

Snug with their mommy,
the rabbits are all
Tumbled together
in one furry ball.

Cozy and warm,
they will sleep safe and sound,
Curled in their bed
on the soft, mossy ground.

Rocked by the waves
beneath velvet blue skies,
Wrapped in her mommy's arms,
small otter lies.

Under the stars
in the dappled moonlight,
"One kiss," smiles mommy,
"and then it's sleep-tight."

Snowflakes are swirling,
all fluffy and white,
Sparkling like stars in the
gleaming moonlight.

Cuddled up close,
little penguin stays warm,
Through the cold frosty night,
till the first light of dawn.

As mother owl hoots
her sweet low lullaby,
Her baby owls blink
at the star-studded sky.

Through the dark treetops,
her echoing call
Sings to the world,
"Goodnight to you all!"

Baby whale drifts
to the deep ocean's song,
Close to his mother,
all the night long.

Down through the water
the soft moonlight streams,
As little whale floats
in a sea of sweet dreams.

Small panda sleeps
as the stars peek-a-boo,
Held by his mother
all the night through.

Cuddled up close,
she gives him a kiss.
Tucked in together,
they're perfect like this.

Sleep, my child, sleep,
'neath the moon's silver light.
I love you, sleepyhead,
sweet dreams—goodnight!